Harrison P. Spader, PERSONAL SPACE INVADER

written by **Christianne Jones**
pictures by **Cale Atkinson**

PICTURE WINDOW BOOKS
a capstone imprint

To my godchildren — Emma, Aubree, Elsa, Landon, and Violet
You can always invade my space. –christianne

To my favorite space invader, Jessika. –cale

Harrison P. Spader, Personal Space Invader
is published by Picture Window Books, a Capstone imprint
1710 Roe Crest Drive , North Mankato, Minnesota 56003
www.mycapstone.com

Library of Congress Cataloging-in-Publication Data will be available
on the Library of Congress website.

ISBN: 978-1-5158-2722-1 (hardcover)
ISBN: 978-1-5158-3455-7 (paperback)

Designer: Lori Bye

Printed in the United States of America.
PA021

Harrison P. Spader loved life and wanted to share his love with everyone.

However, Harrison's overly joyful
ways were causing problems.

When Harrison was little, it wasn't a big deal.
But the problem grew every year.

He sat a little too close.

Shook hands a little too long.

High-fived a little too hard.

And hugged a little too much.

And Harrison definitely did NOT know the definition of a close talker!

Harrison P. Spader was a
Personal Space Invader.

There was that time when Harrison played center field — kind of.

And that other time when he went "swimming" with his friends.

And who could forget the bus ride to the zoo
or story time at the library?

His family was used to being smothered in love.
They were just that type of family.

But after calls from teachers, coaches, and other parents, Harrison's dad knew he had to have a talk with Harrison.

"Harrison, I hear you are having trouble
staying in your own space," his dad said.

"Not really. I don't need much space," Harrison replied.

"But other people need their space," his dad reasoned.

"When I was your age, my mom taught me something called the Space Saver," his dad said. "It's really simple."

Arms out front

then out real wide.

Now place your arms

back by your sides.

"If you can do the Space Saver without touching anyone, you have left a good amount of space," his dad told him.

Harrison and his dad practiced the
Space Saver over and over and over.

By the end of the night, the entire family was doing it.

The next day, Harrison used the Space Saver
every chance he could. He loved it!

Harrison even used it when he didn't need to,
which he thought was extra clever.

However, his teacher and friends weren't as impressed.

After another phone call, Harrison's dad had a few reminders about personal space.

"I know you like the **Space Saver**, but sometimes it might be too crowded for it. Then just put your arms down, be still, and try to stay in your own space," his dad said.

"Got it, Dad!" Harrison replied.

And Harrison really did get it this time!
On the bus ride to school the next day, Harrison
wanted to squish in a seat with two of his friends.

But Harrison found himself a seat with some space instead. And that was just the beginning!

At his next baseball game,
Harrison really did play center field.

When he went swimming with his friends,
he brought his own tube.

And during story time, he actually sat on his own mat and didn't move it closer to anyone! This took extra restraint for Harrison, but he did it.

Harrison didn't get it right all of the time.
After all, nobody's perfect, and leaving personal space
can be tricky — especially when you love life
as much as Harrison does.

But Harrison got it right most of the time,
and that was a relief to everyone!